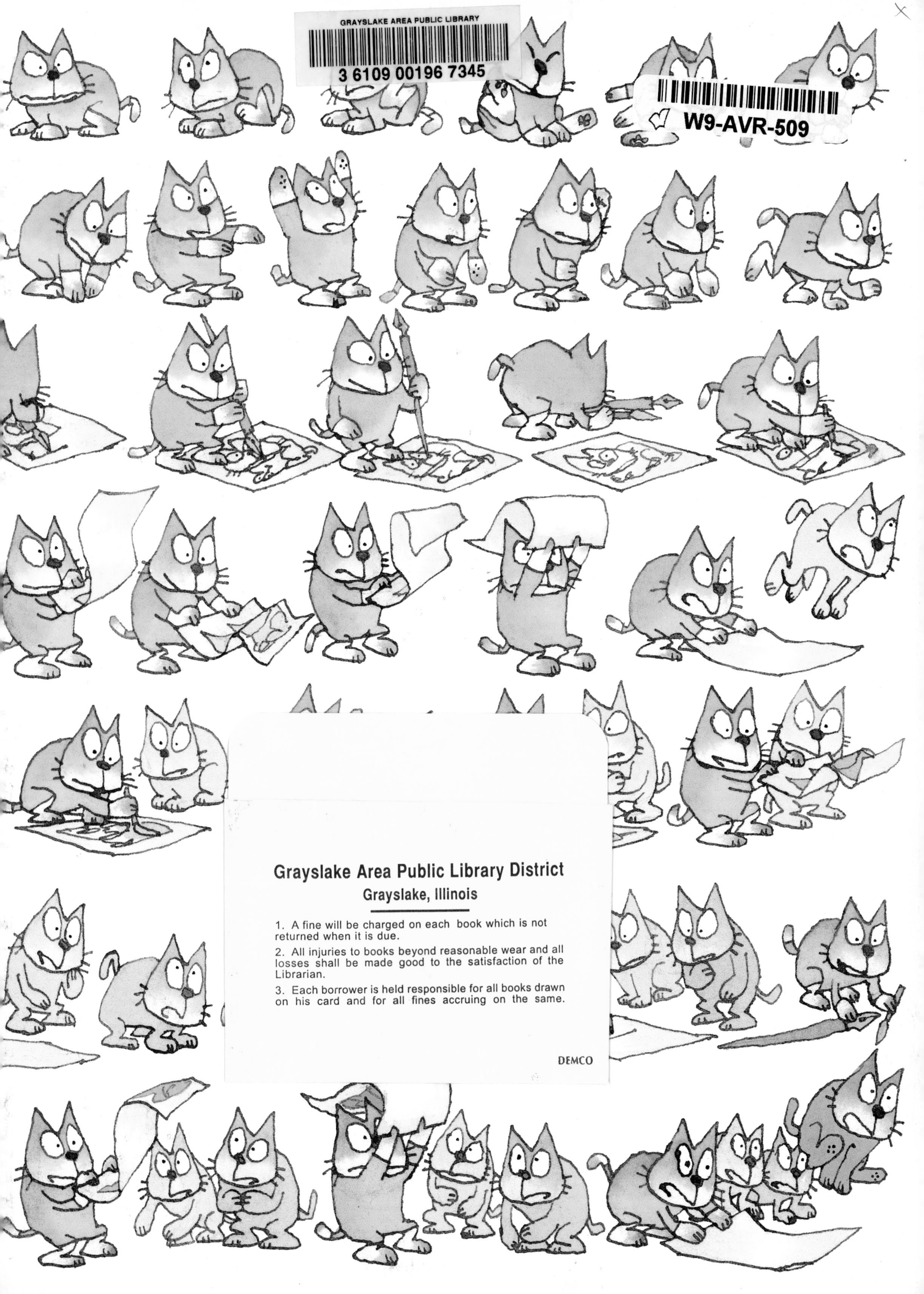

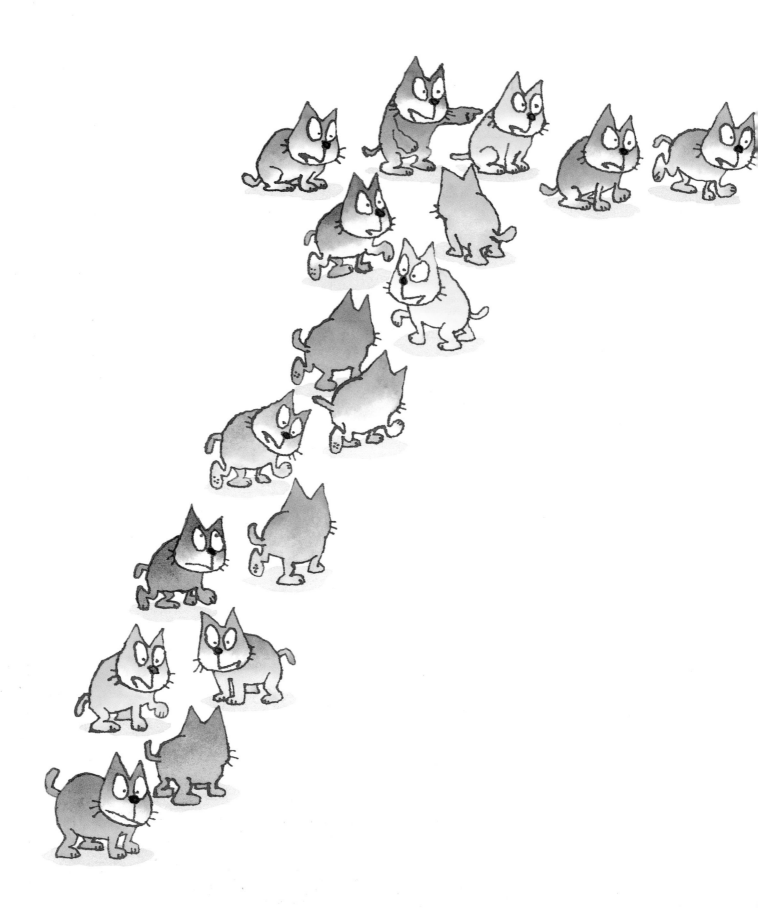

COMIC ADVENTURES OF BOOTS

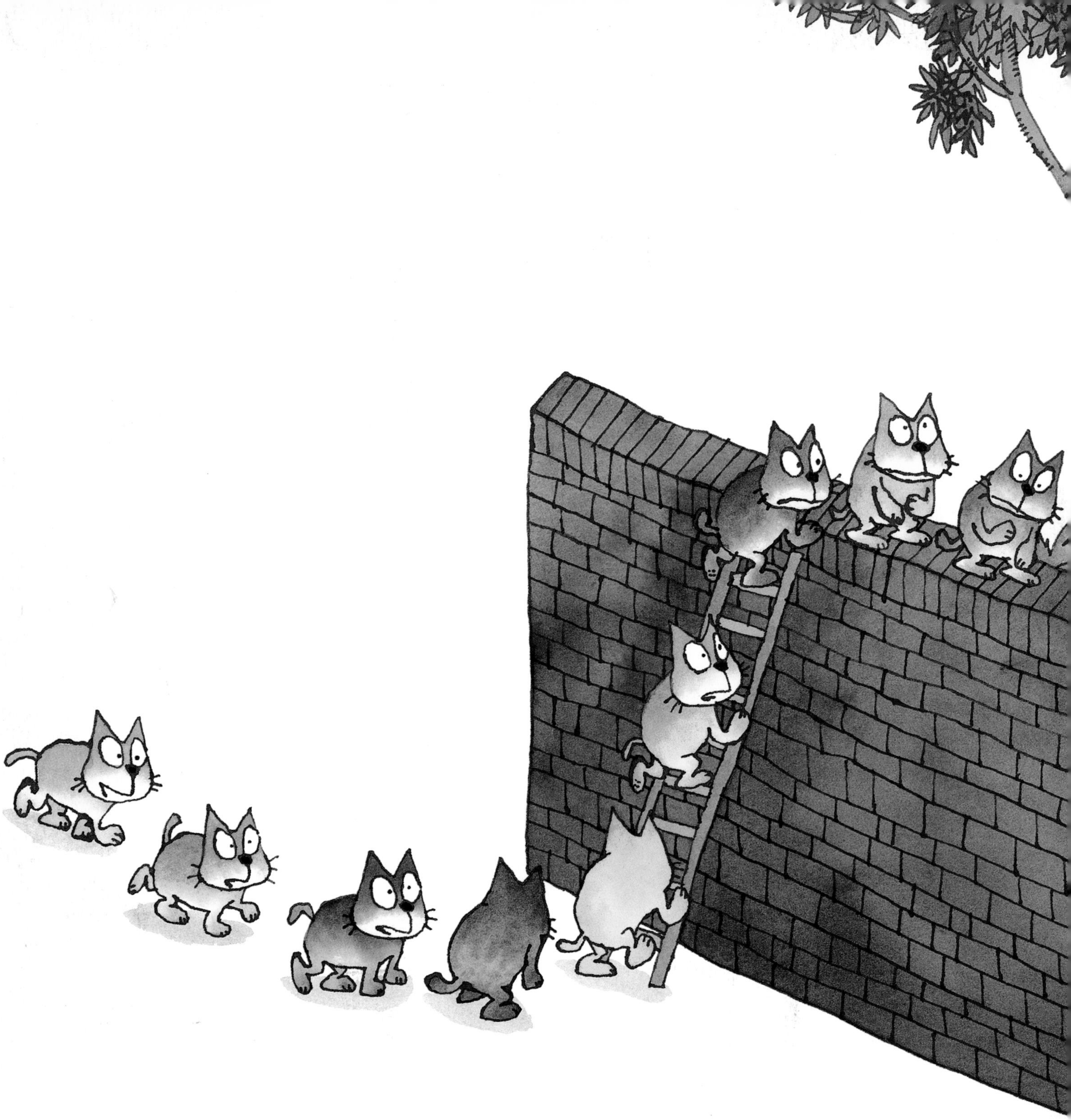

First published in Great Britain by Andersen Press Ltd., 2002
Library of Congress Control Number: 2001098411
Color separations by Fotoriproduzioni Grafiche, Verona, Italy
Printed and bound in Italy by Grafiche AZ, Verona
First American edition, 2002
10 9 8 7 6 5 4 3 2 1

COMIC ADVENTURES OF BOOTS

SATOSHI KITAMURA

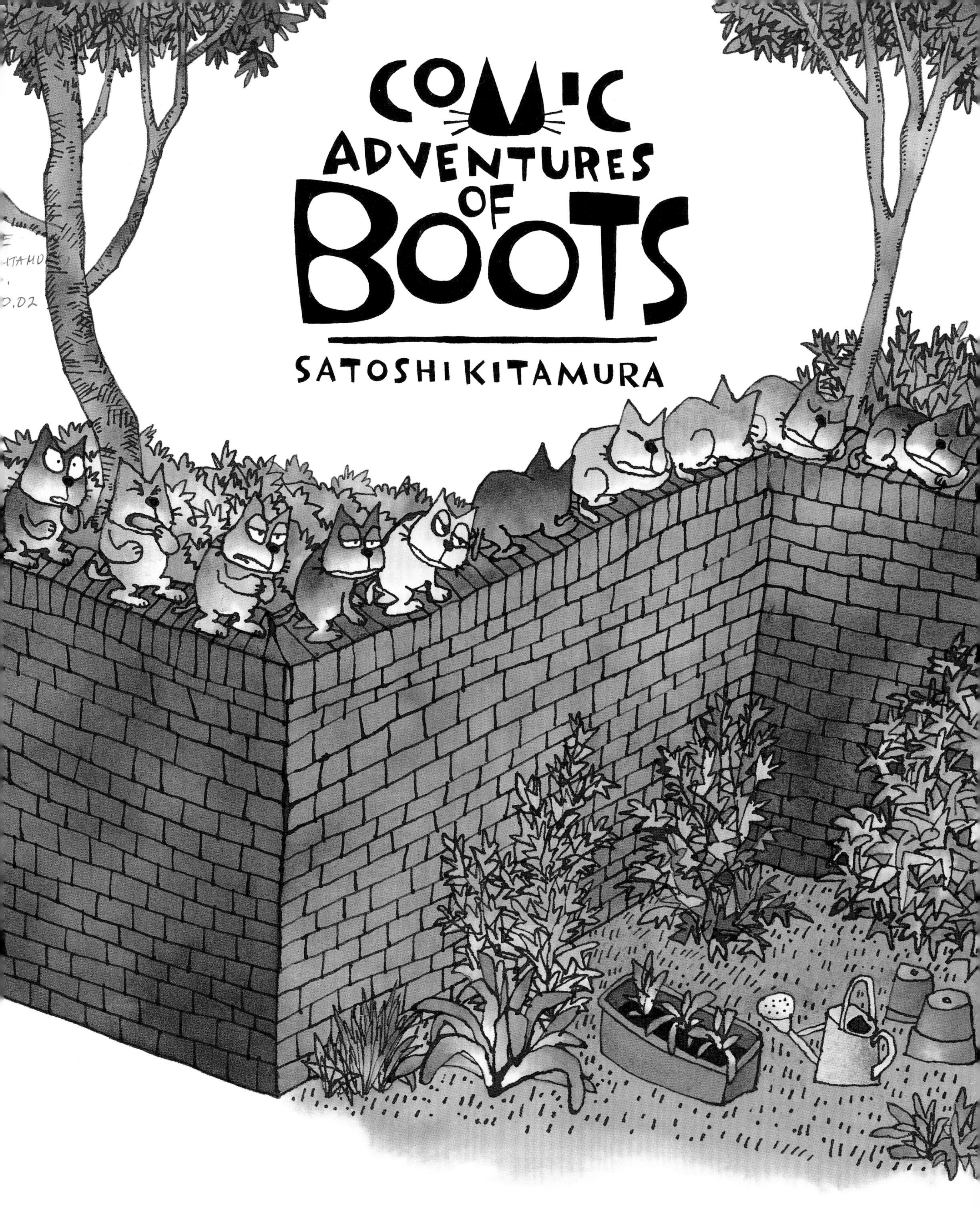

FARRAR STRAUS GIROUX
NEW YORK

OPERATION FISH BISCUIT

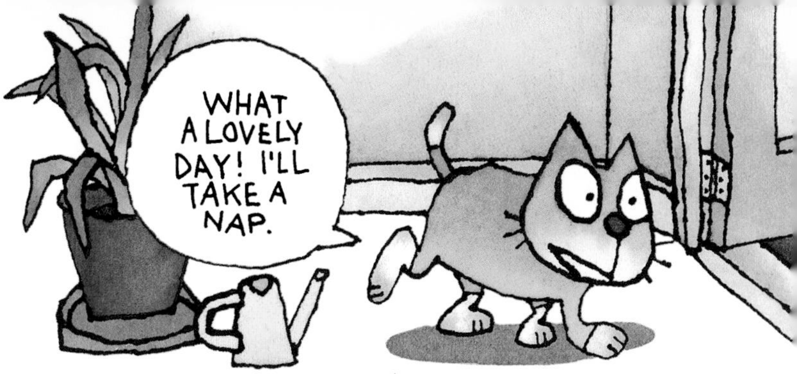
WHAT A LOVELY DAY! I'LL TAKE A NAP.

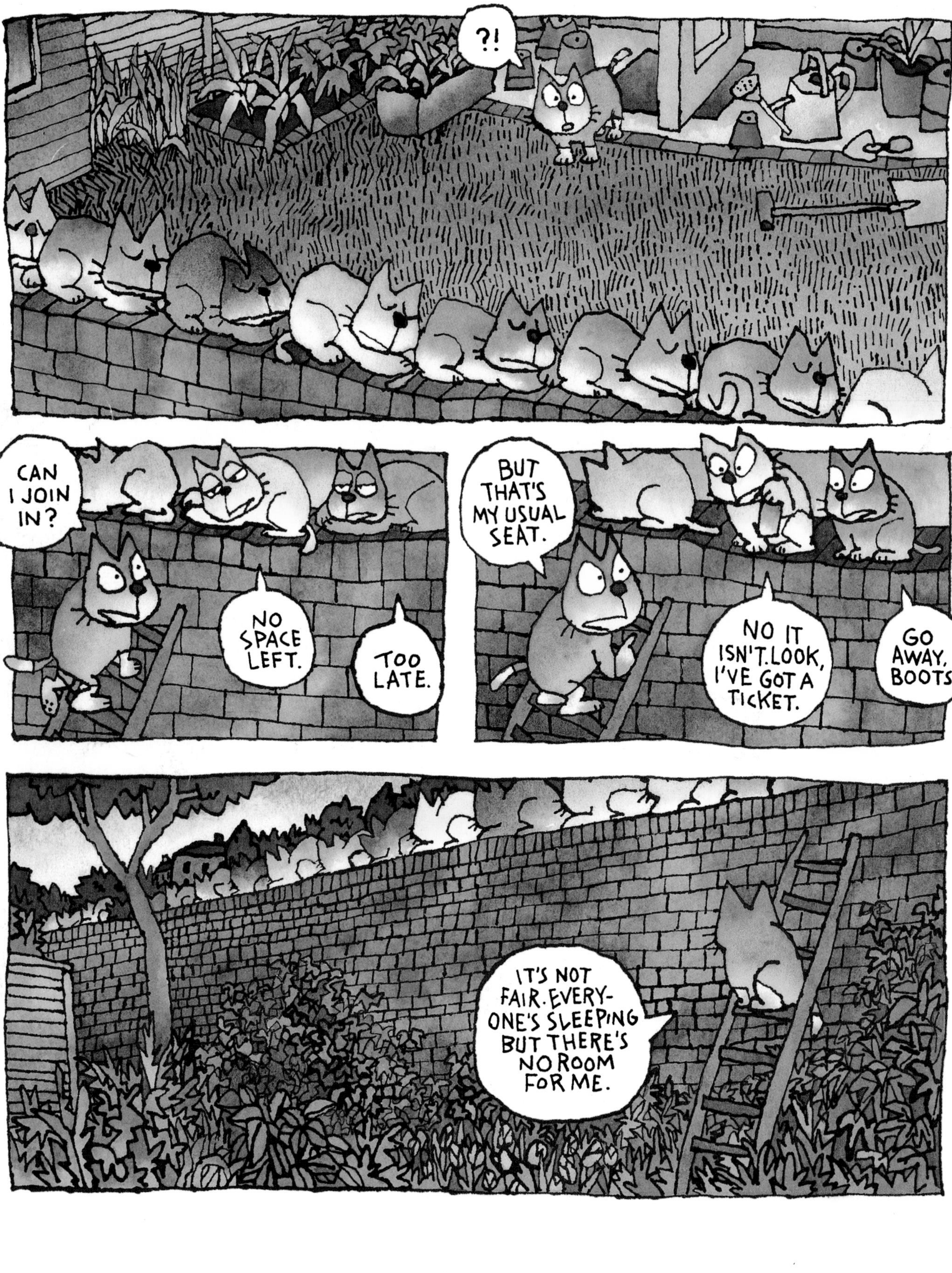
?!
CAN I JOIN IN?
NO SPACE LEFT.
TOO LATE.
BUT THAT'S MY USUAL SEAT.
NO IT ISN'T. LOOK, I'VE GOT A TICKET.
GO AWAY, BOOTS.
IT'S NOT FAIR. EVERY-ONE'S SLEEPING BUT THERE'S NO ROOM FOR ME.

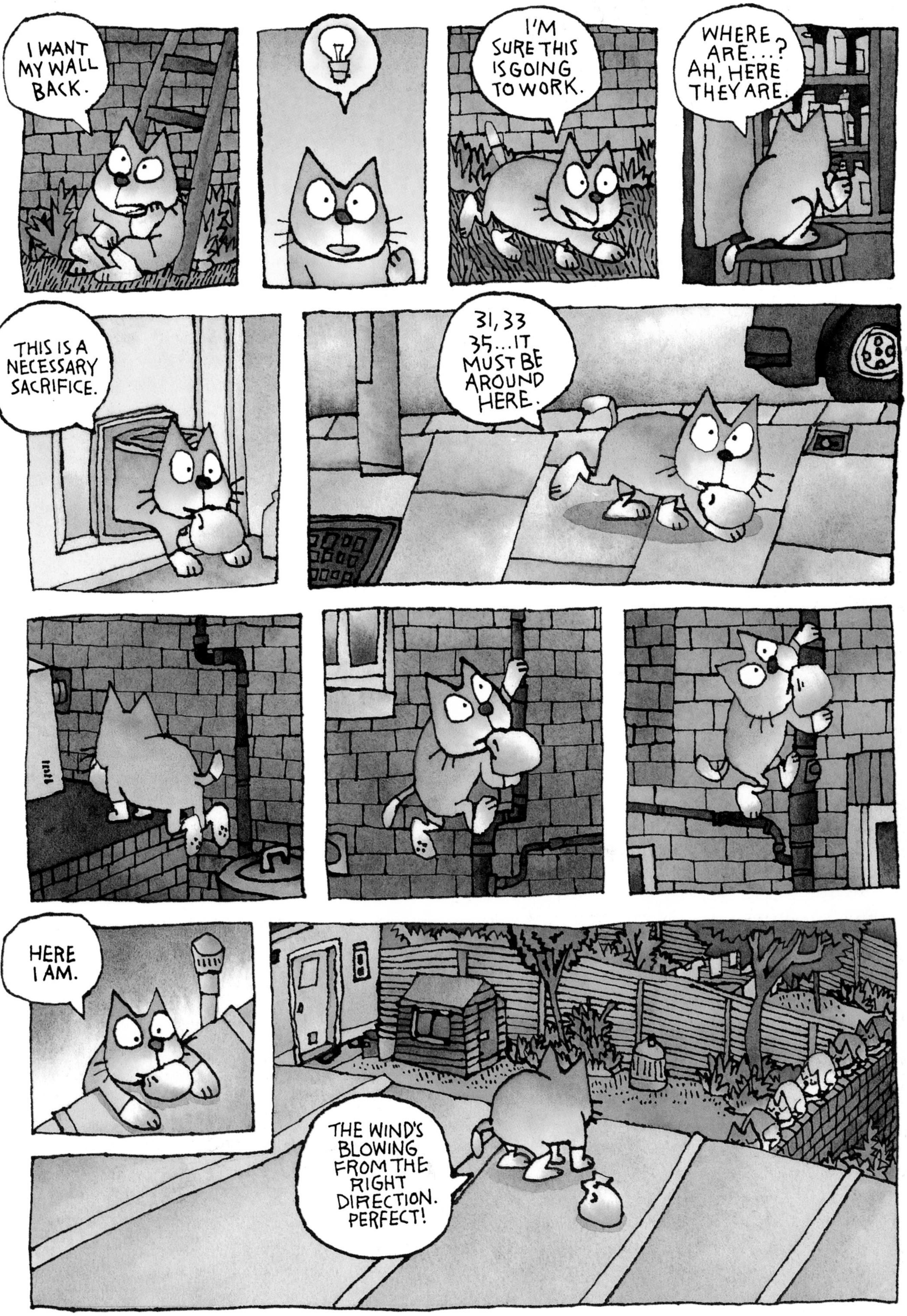
I WANT MY WALL BACK.
I'M SURE THIS IS GOING TO WORK.
WHERE ARE...? AH, HERE THEY ARE.
THIS IS A NECESSARY SACRIFICE.
31, 33 35... IT MUST BE AROUND HERE.
HERE I AM.
THE WIND'S BLOWING FROM THE RIGHT DIRECTION. PERFECT!

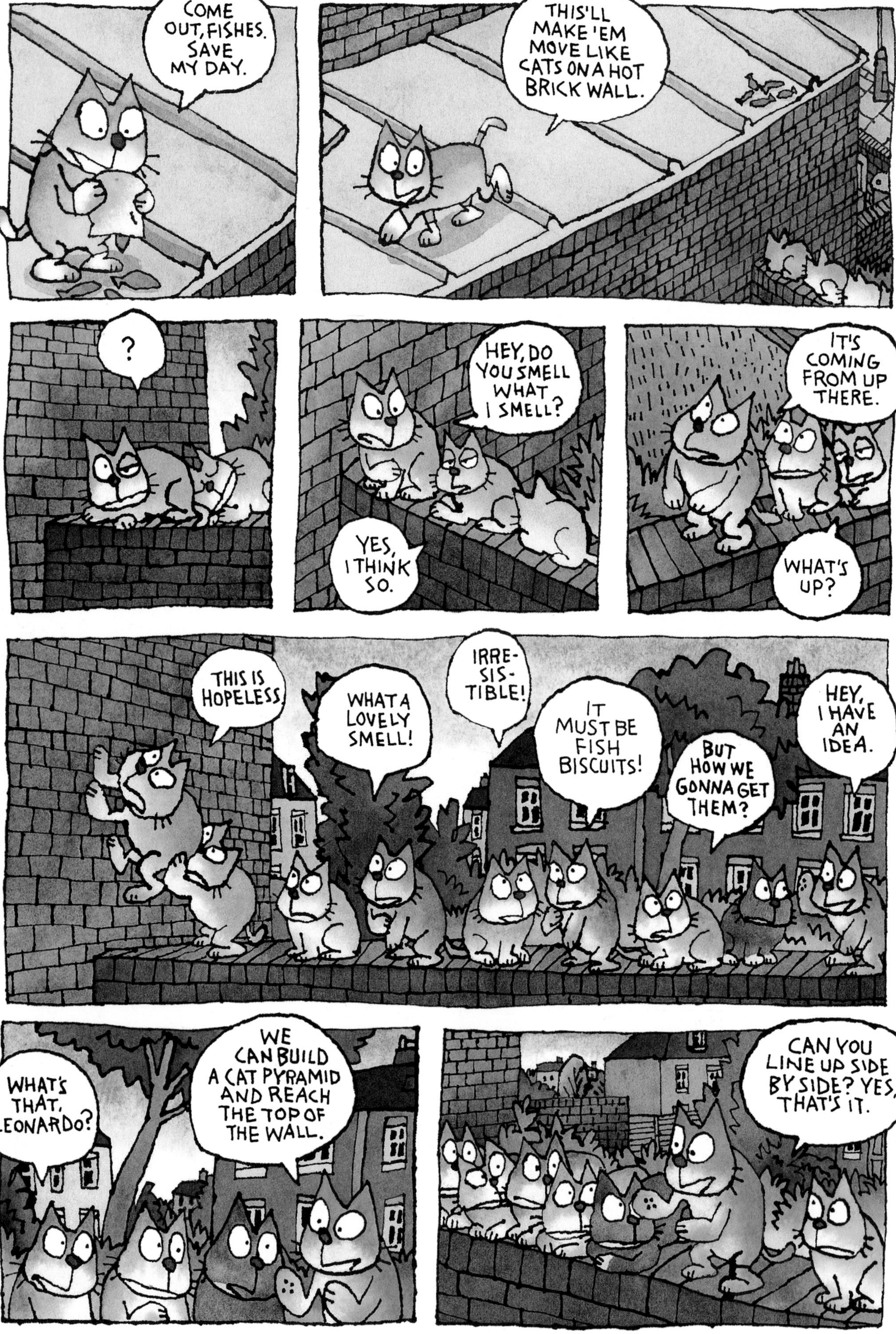
COME OUT, FISHES. SAVE MY DAY.
THIS'LL MAKE 'EM MOVE LIKE CATS ON A HOT BRICK WALL.
?
HEY, DO YOU SMELL WHAT I SMELL?
YES, I THINK SO.
IT'S COMING FROM UP THERE.
WHAT'S UP?
THIS IS HOPELESS.
WHAT A LOVELY SMELL!
IRRE-SIS-TIBLE!
IT MUST BE FISH BISCUITS!
BUT HOW WE GONNA GET THEM?
HEY, I HAVE AN IDEA.
WHAT'S THAT, LEONARDO?
WE CAN BUILD A CAT PYRAMID AND REACH THE TOP OF THE WALL.
CAN YOU LINE UP SIDE BY SIDE? YES, THAT'S IT.

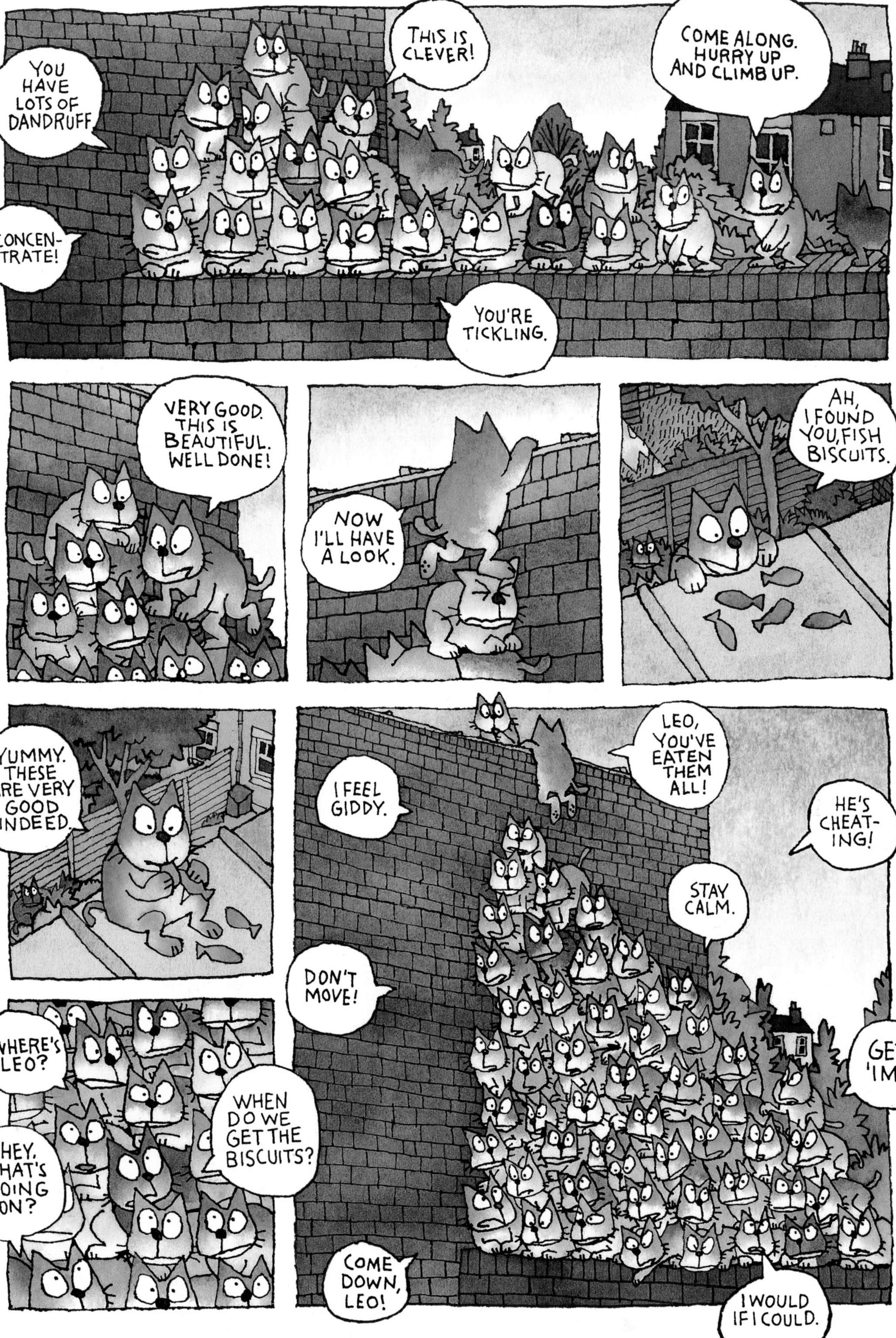
YOU HAVE LOTS OF DANDRUFF.
CONCENTRATE!
THIS IS CLEVER!
COME ALONG. HURRY UP AND CLIMB UP.
YOU'RE TICKLING.
VERY GOOD. THIS IS BEAUTIFUL. WELL DONE!
NOW I'LL HAVE A LOOK.
AH, I FOUND YOU, FISH BISCUITS.
YUMMY. THESE ARE VERY GOOD INDEED.
WHERE'S LEO?
WHEN DO WE GET THE BISCUITS?
HEY. WHAT'S GOING ON?
I FEEL GIDDY.
LEO, YOU'VE EATEN THEM ALL!
HE'S CHEATING!
STAY CALM.
DON'T MOVE!
GET 'IM!
COME DOWN, LEO!
I WOULD IF I COULD.

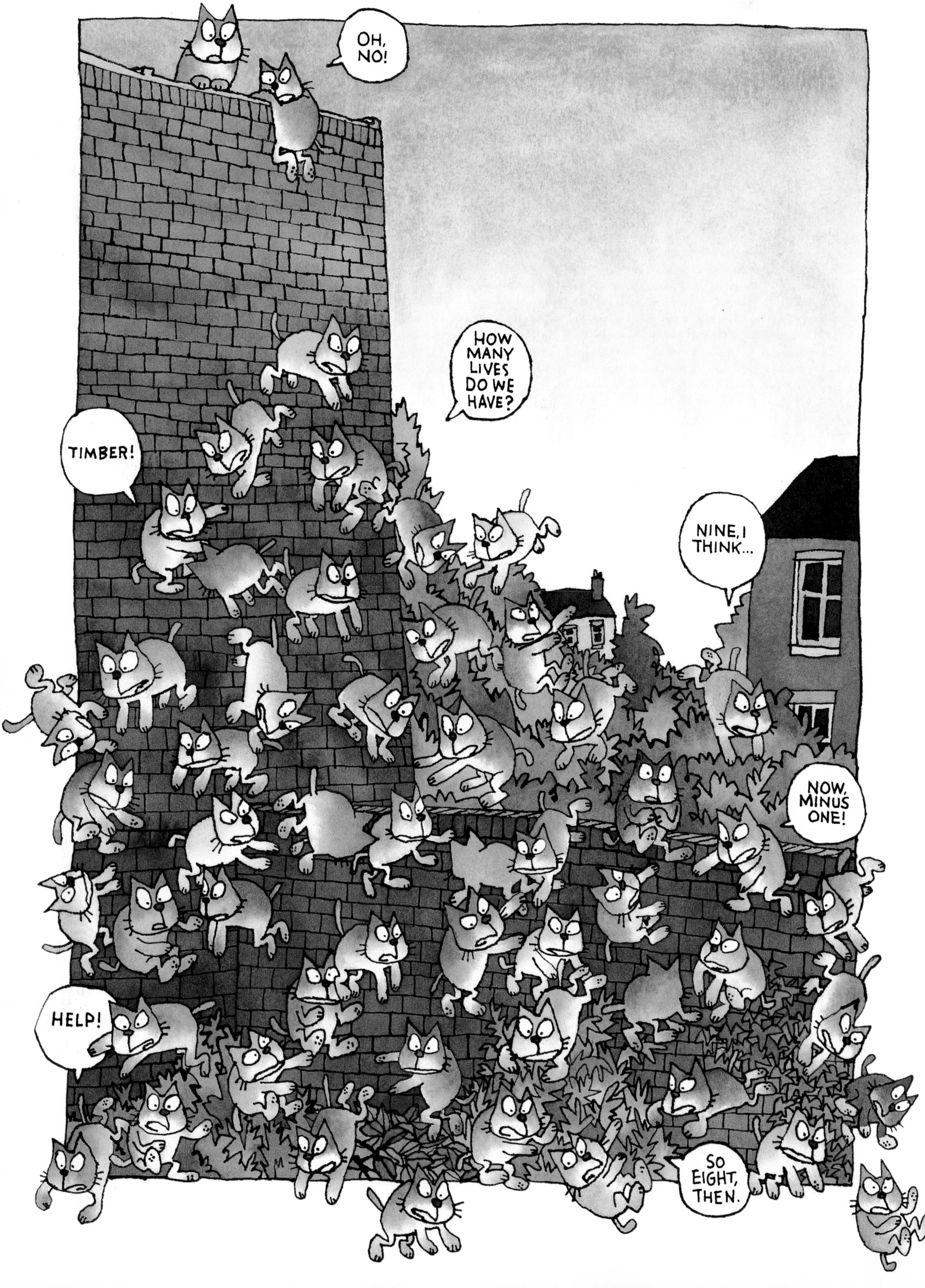
OH, NO!
HOW MANY LIVES DO WE HAVE?
TIMBER!
NINE, I THINK...
NOW, MINUS ONE!
HELP!
SO EIGHT, THEN.

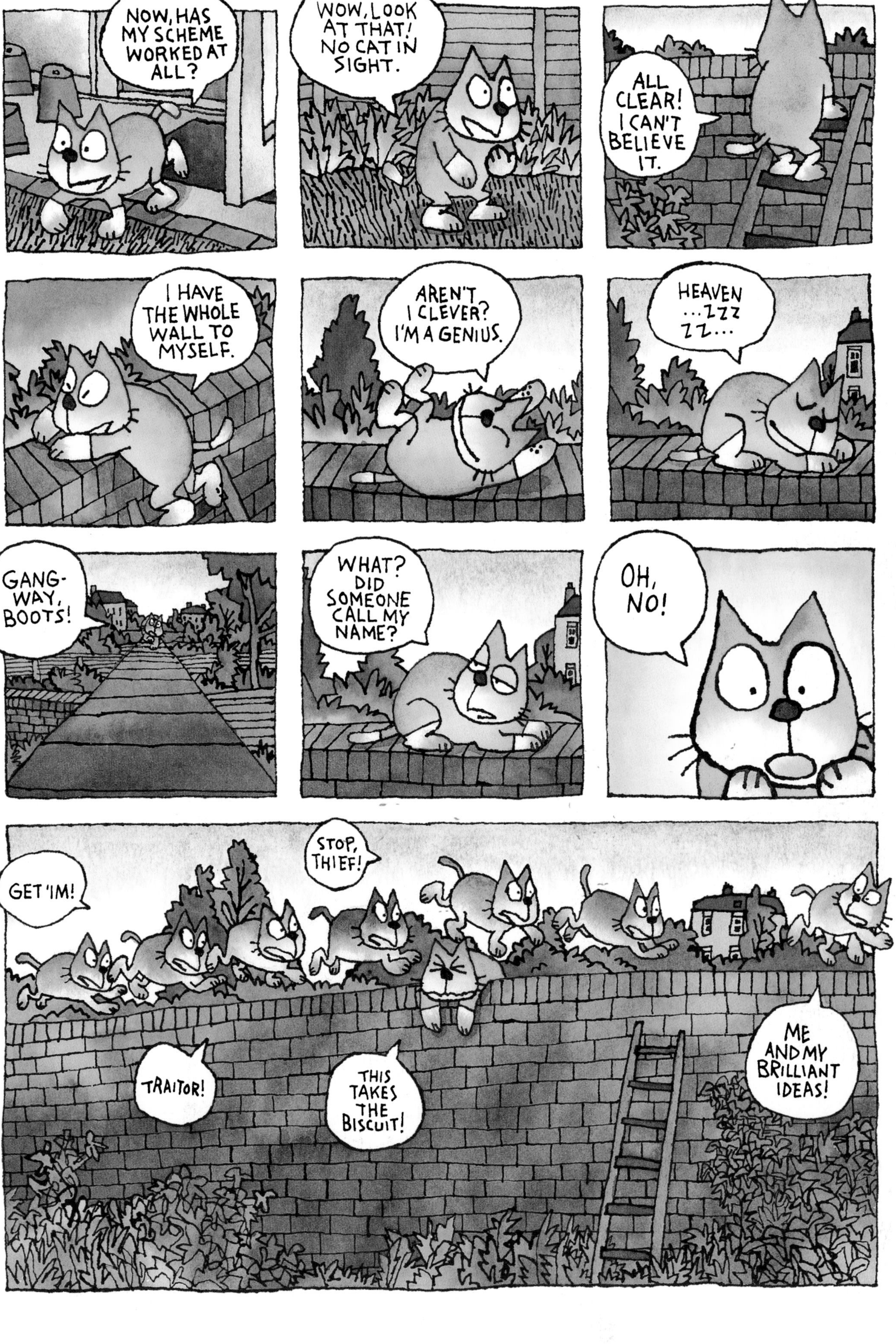
NOW, HAS MY SCHEME WORKED AT ALL?
WOW, LOOK AT THAT! NO CAT IN SIGHT.
ALL CLEAR! I CAN'T BELIEVE IT.
I HAVE THE WHOLE WALL TO MYSELF.
AREN'T I CLEVER? I'M A GENIUS.
HEAVEN ...ZZZ ZZ...
GANG-WAY, BOOTS!
WHAT? DID SOMEONE CALL MY NAME?
OH, NO!
GET 'IM!
STOP, THIEF!
TRAITOR!
THIS TAKES THE BISCUIT!
ME AND MY BRILLIANT IDEAS!

PLEASED TO MEET YOU, MADAM QUARK

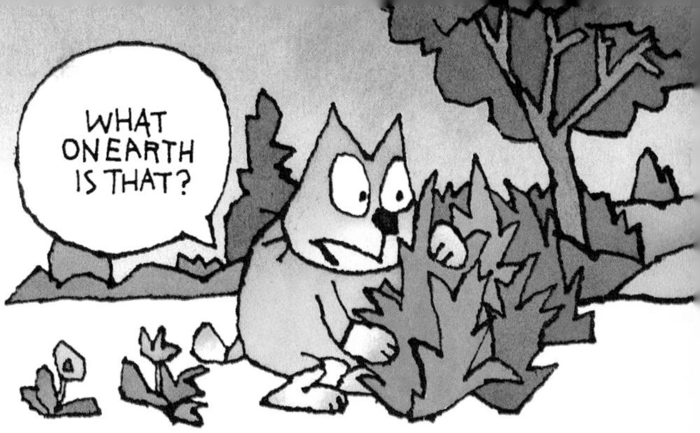
WHAT ON EARTH IS THAT?

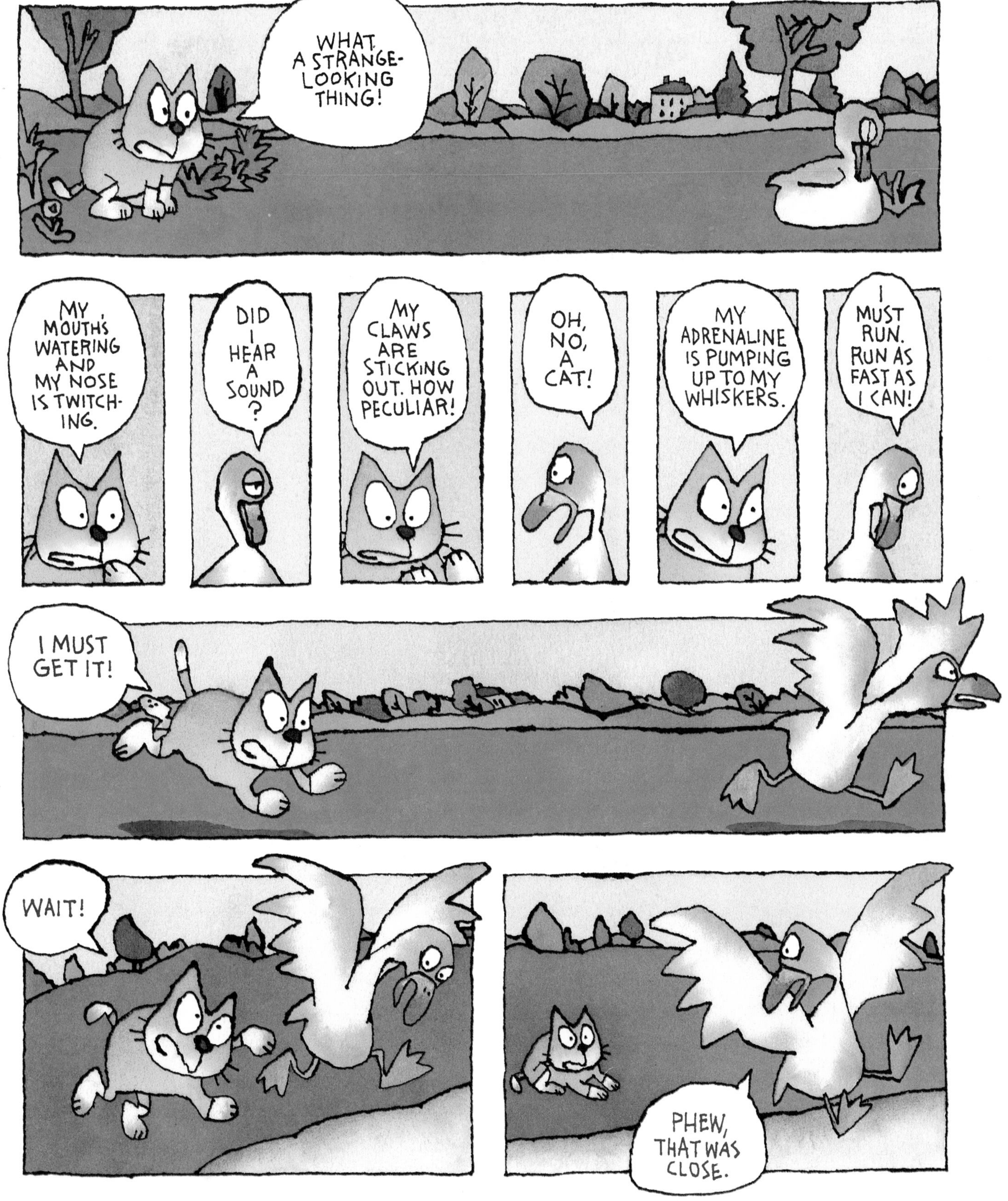
WHAT A STRANGE-LOOKING THING!
MY MOUTH'S WATERING AND MY NOSE IS TWITCHING.
DID I HEAR A SOUND?
MY CLAWS ARE STICKING OUT. HOW PECULIAR!
OH, NO, A CAT!
MY ADRENALINE IS PUMPING UP TO MY WHISKERS.
I MUST RUN. RUN AS FAST AS I CAN!
I MUST GET IT!
WAIT!
PHEW, THAT WAS CLOSE.

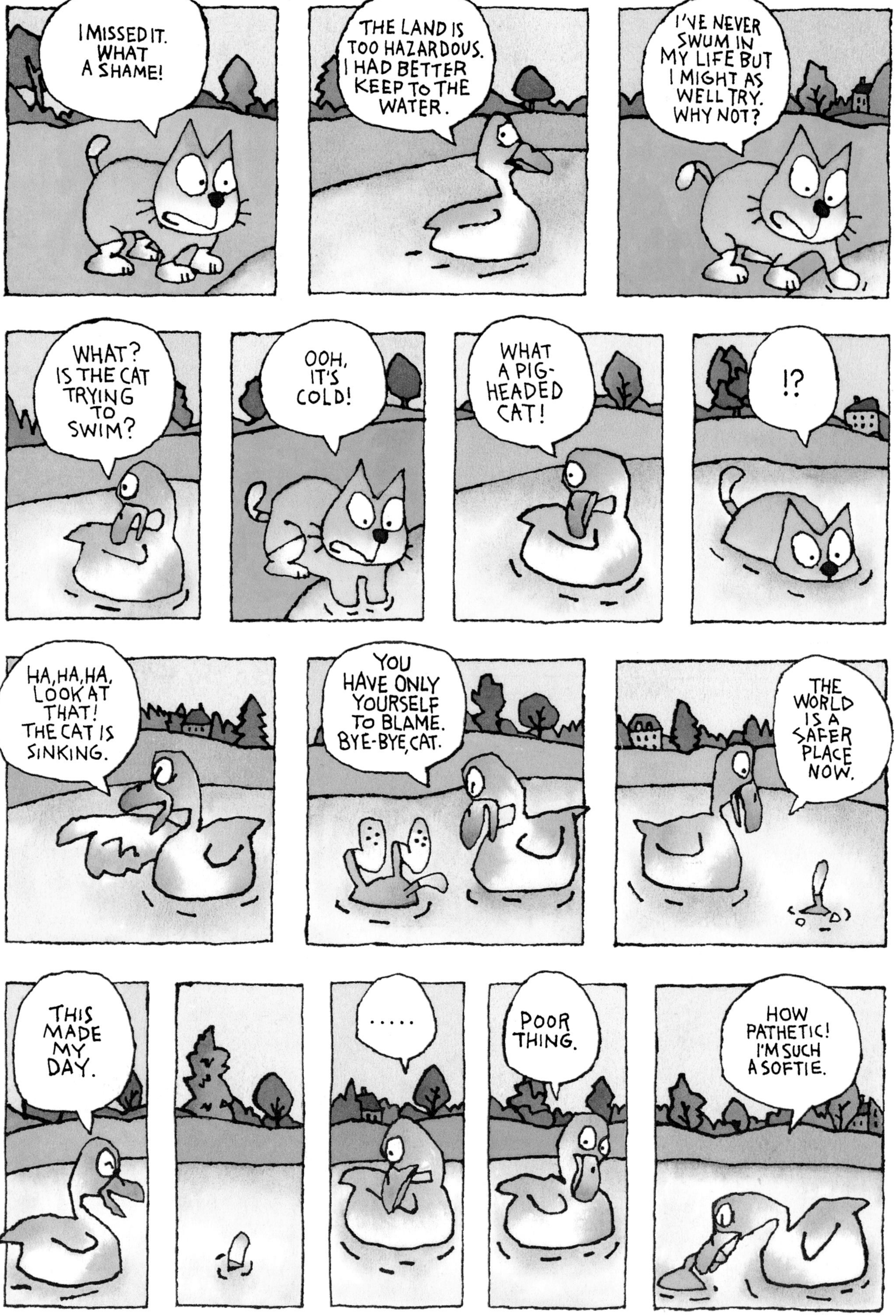
I MISSED IT. WHAT A SHAME!
THE LAND IS TOO HAZARDOUS. I HAD BETTER KEEP TO THE WATER.
I'VE NEVER SWUM IN MY LIFE BUT I MIGHT AS WELL TRY. WHY NOT?
WHAT? IS THE CAT TRYING TO SWIM?
OOH, IT'S COLD!
WHAT A PIG-HEADED CAT!
!?
HA, HA, HA, LOOK AT THAT! THE CAT IS SINKING.
YOU HAVE ONLY YOURSELF TO BLAME. BYE-BYE, CAT.
THE WORLD IS A SAFER PLACE NOW.
THIS MADE MY DAY.
.....
POOR THING.
HOW PATHETIC! I'M SUCH A SOFTIE.

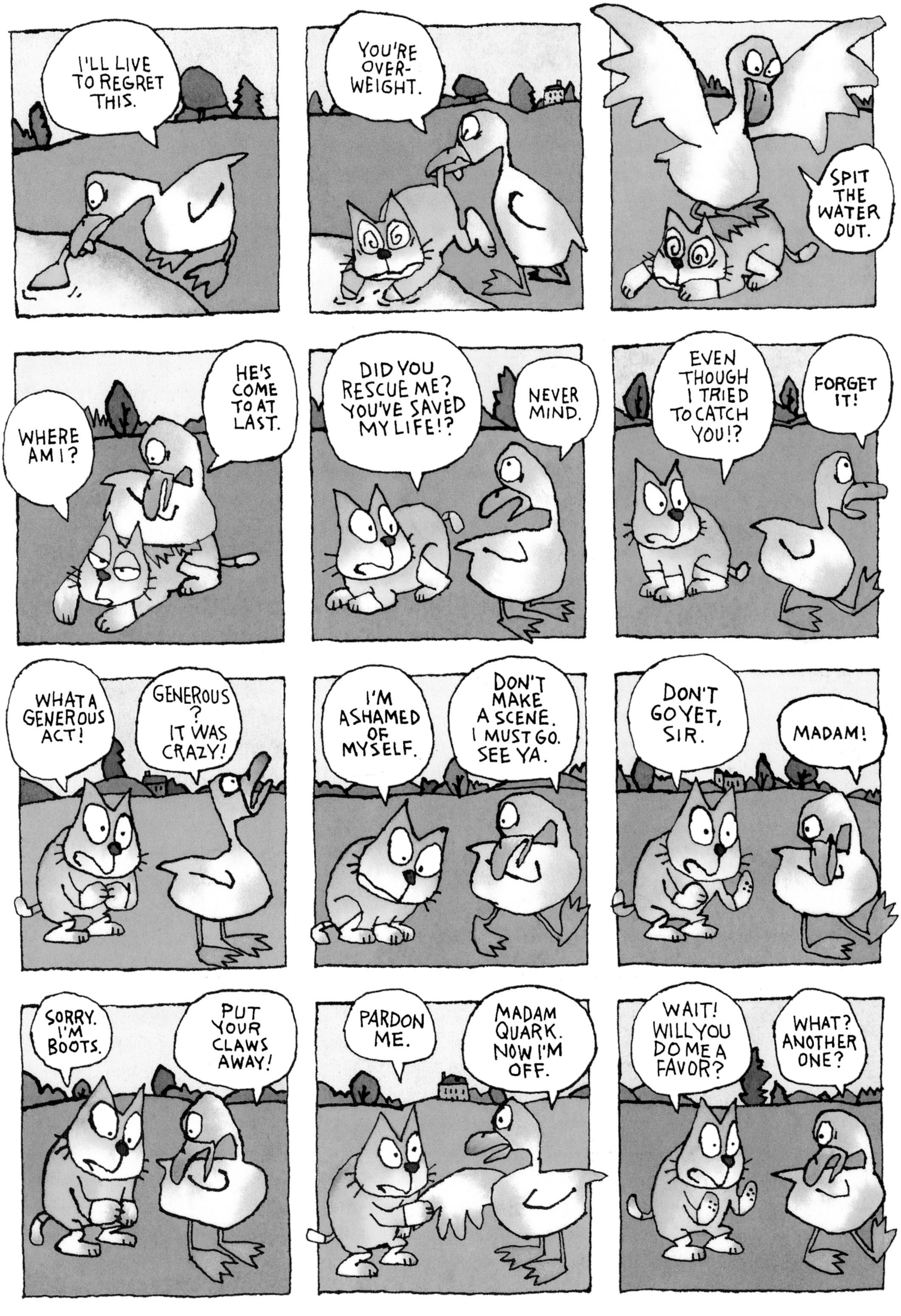
I'LL LIVE TO REGRET THIS.
YOU'RE OVER-WEIGHT.
SPIT THE WATER OUT.
WHERE AM I?
HE'S COME TO AT LAST.
DID YOU RESCUE ME? YOU'VE SAVED MY LIFE!?
NEVER MIND.
EVEN THOUGH I TRIED TO CATCH YOU!?
FORGET IT!
WHAT A GENEROUS ACT!
GENEROUS? IT WAS CRAZY!
I'M ASHAMED OF MYSELF.
DON'T MAKE A SCENE. I MUST GO. SEE YA.
DON'T GO YET, SIR.
MADAM!
SORRY. I'M BOOTS.
PUT YOUR CLAWS AWAY!
PARDON ME.
MADAM QUARK. NOW I'M OFF.
WAIT! WILL YOU DO ME A FAVOR?
WHAT? ANOTHER ONE?

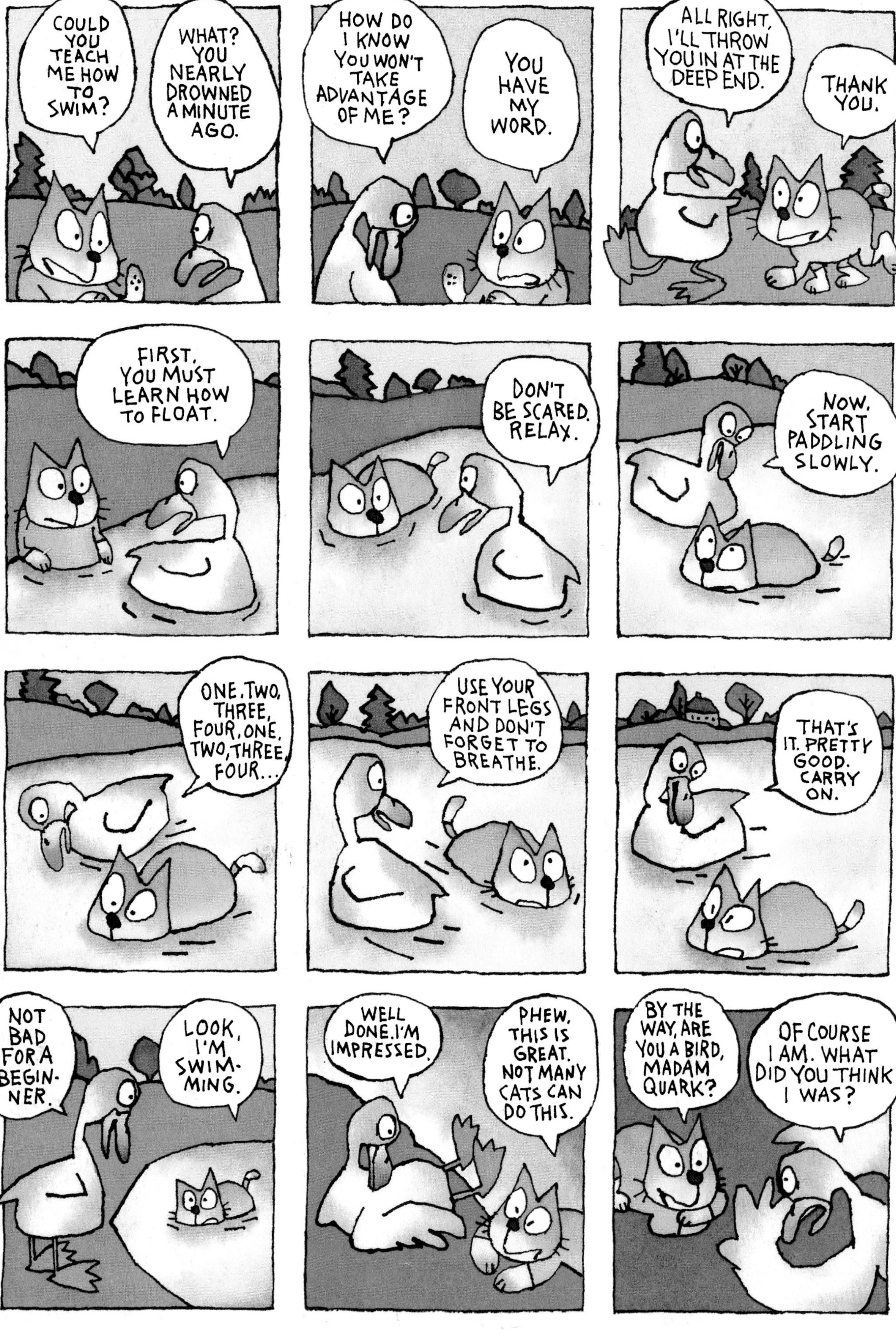
COULD YOU TEACH ME HOW TO SWIM?
WHAT? YOU NEARLY DROWNED A MINUTE AGO.
HOW DO I KNOW YOU WON'T TAKE ADVANTAGE OF ME?
YOU HAVE MY WORD.
ALL RIGHT, I'LL THROW YOU IN AT THE DEEP END.
THANK YOU.
FIRST, YOU MUST LEARN HOW TO FLOAT.
DON'T BE SCARED. RELAX.
NOW, START PADDLING SLOWLY.
ONE, TWO, THREE, FOUR, ONE, TWO, THREE, FOUR...
USE YOUR FRONT LEGS AND DON'T FORGET TO BREATHE.
THAT'S IT. PRETTY GOOD. CARRY ON.
NOT BAD FOR A BEGIN-NER.
LOOK, I'M SWIM-MING.
WELL DONE. I'M IMPRESSED.
PHEW, THIS IS GREAT. NOT MANY CATS CAN DO THIS.
BY THE WAY, ARE YOU A BIRD, MADAM QUARK?
OF COURSE I AM. WHAT DID YOU THINK I WAS?

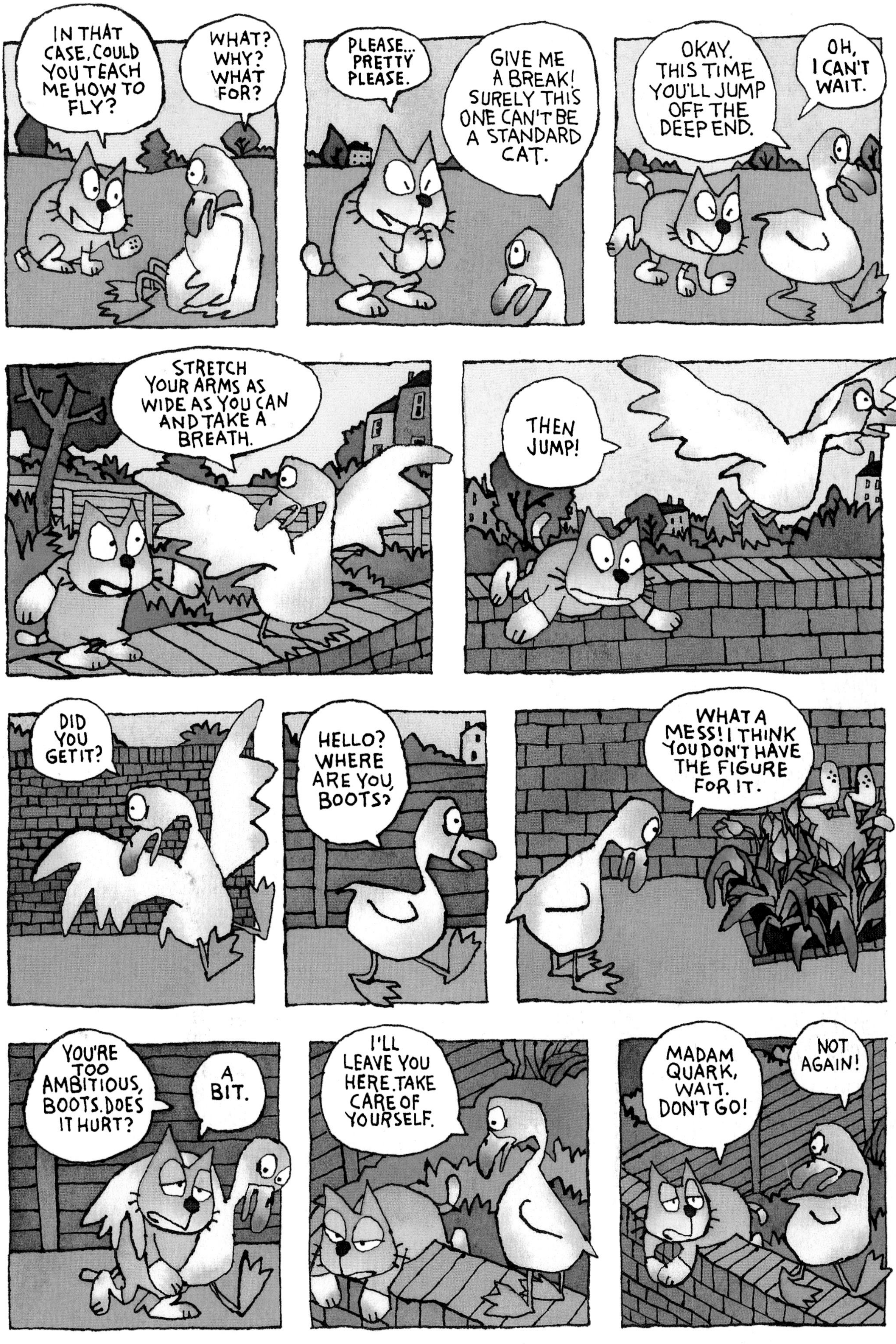
IN THAT CASE, COULD YOU TEACH ME HOW TO FLY?
WHAT? WHY? WHAT FOR?
PLEASE... PRETTY PLEASE.
GIVE ME A BREAK! SURELY THIS ONE CAN'T BE A STANDARD CAT.
OKAY. THIS TIME YOU'LL JUMP OFF THE DEEP END.
OH, I CAN'T WAIT.
STRETCH YOUR ARMS AS WIDE AS YOU CAN AND TAKE A BREATH.
THEN JUMP!
DID YOU GET IT?
HELLO? WHERE ARE YOU, BOOTS?
WHAT A MESS! I THINK YOU DON'T HAVE THE FIGURE FOR IT.
YOU'RE TOO AMBITIOUS, BOOTS. DOES IT HURT?
A BIT.
I'LL LEAVE YOU HERE. TAKE CARE OF YOURSELF.
MADAM QUARK, WAIT. DON'T GO!
NOT AGAIN!

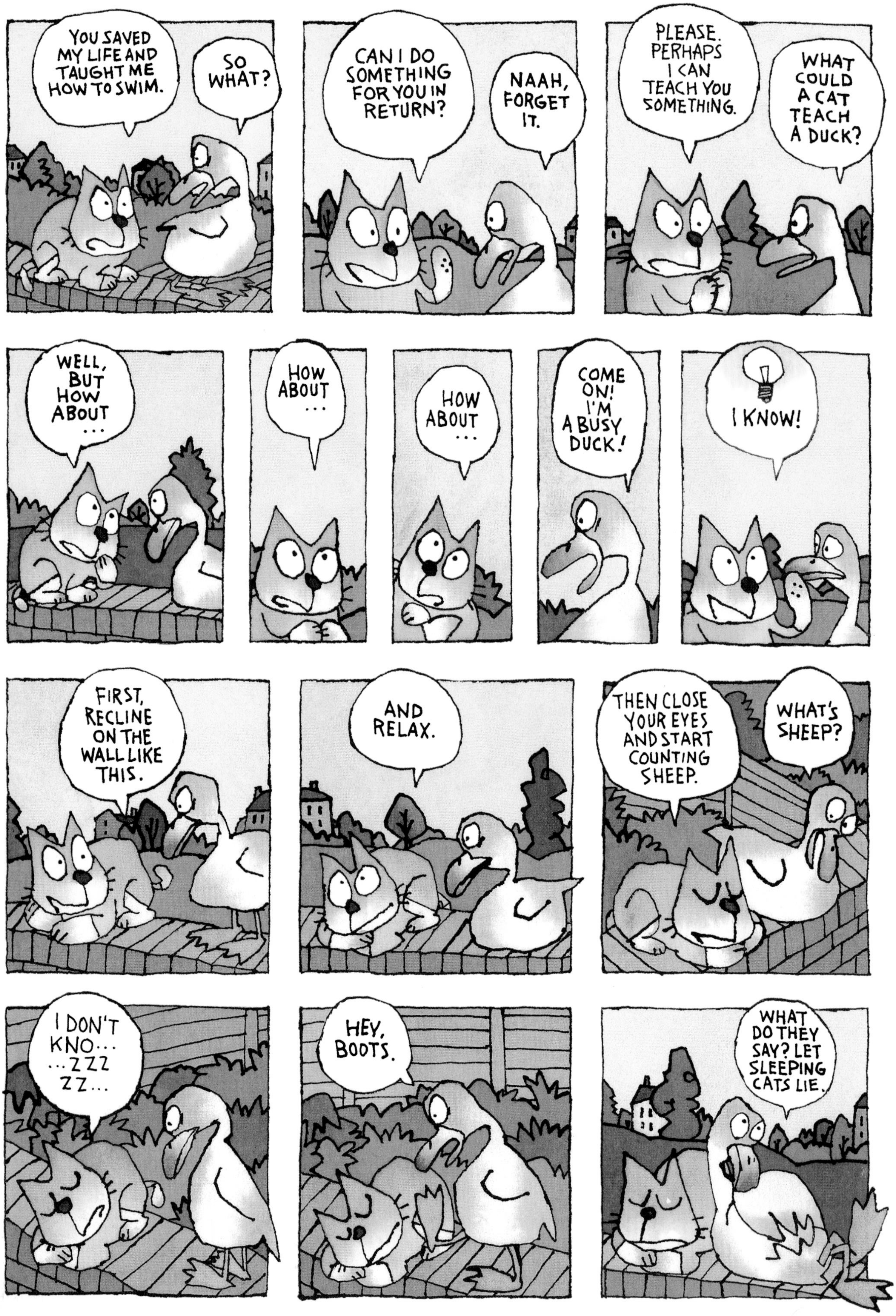
YOU SAVED MY LIFE AND TAUGHT ME HOW TO SWIM.
SO WHAT?
CAN I DO SOMETHING FOR YOU IN RETURN?
NAAH, FORGET IT.
PLEASE. PERHAPS I CAN TEACH YOU SOMETHING.
WHAT COULD A CAT TEACH A DUCK?
WELL, BUT HOW ABOUT . . .
HOW ABOUT . . .
HOW ABOUT . . .
COME ON! I'M A BUSY DUCK!
I KNOW!
FIRST, RECLINE ON THE WALL LIKE THIS.
AND RELAX.
THEN CLOSE YOUR EYES AND START COUNTING SHEEP.
WHAT'S SHEEP?
I DON'T KNO... ...ZZZ ZZ...
HEY, BOOTS.
WHAT DO THEY SAY? LET SLEEPING CATS LIE.

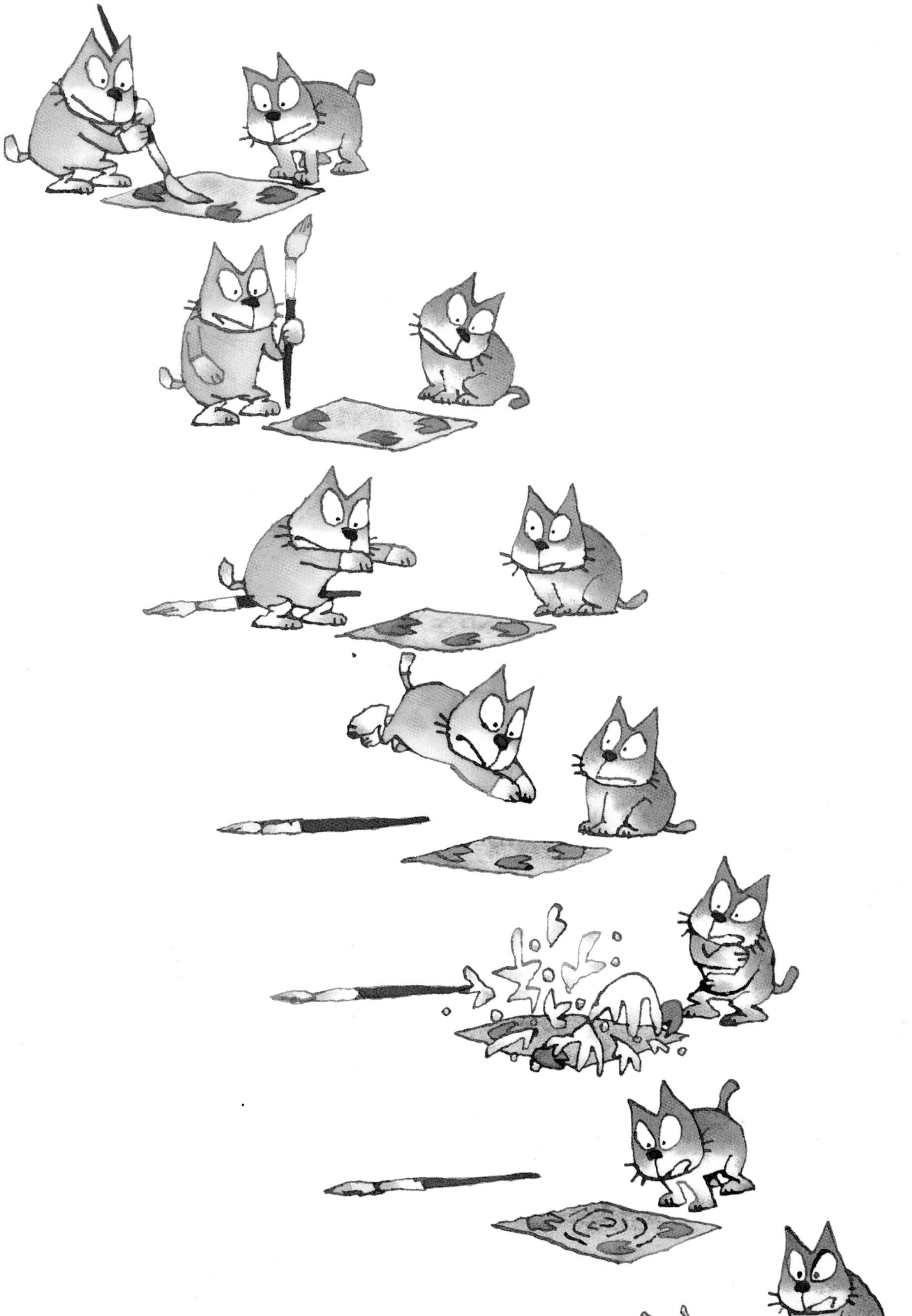

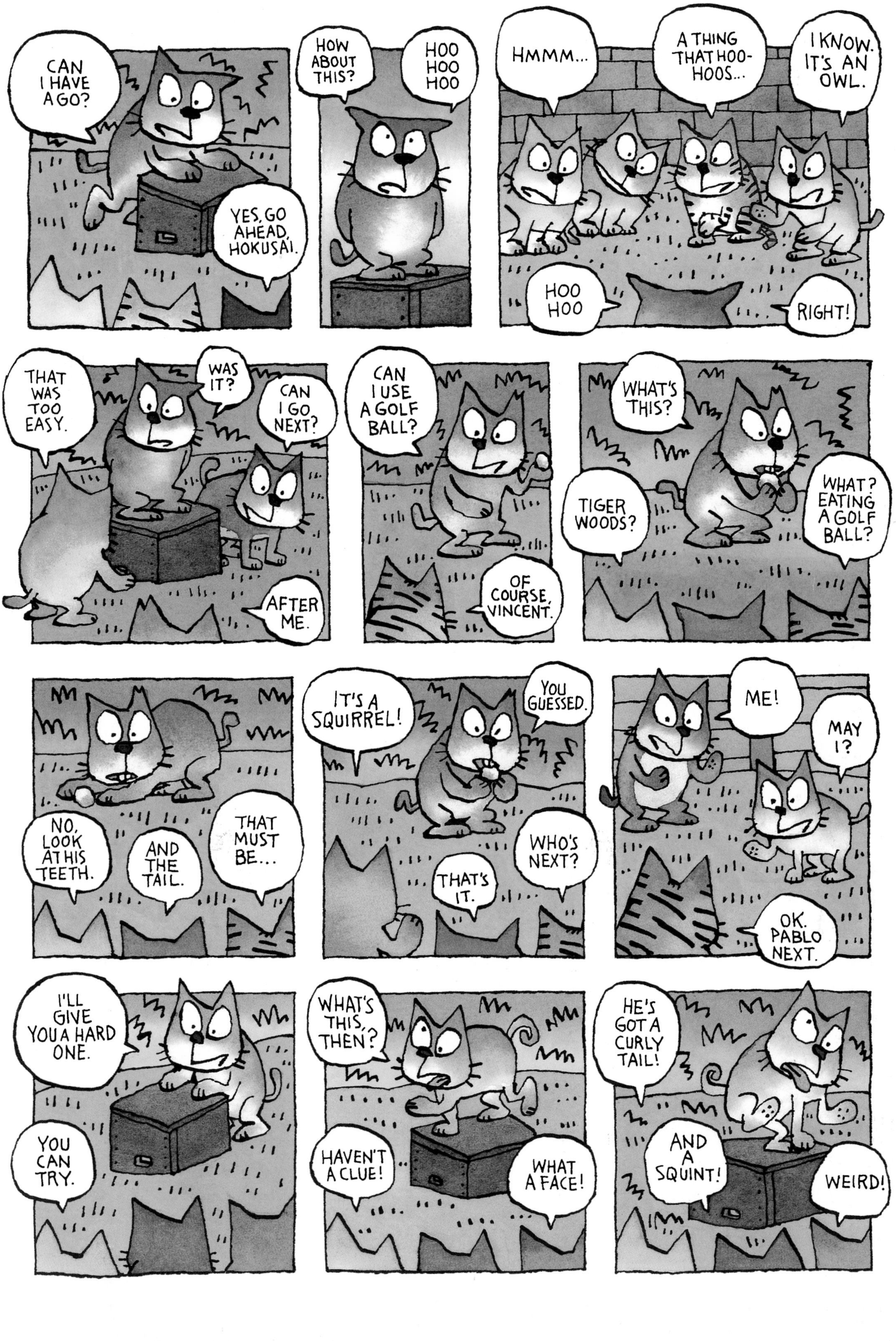
CAN I HAVE A GO?
YES, GO AHEAD, HOKUSAI.
HOW ABOUT THIS?
HOO HOO HOO
HMMM...
A THING THAT HOO-HOOS...
I KNOW. IT'S AN OWL.
HOO HOO
RIGHT!
THAT WAS TOO EASY.
WAS IT?
CAN I GO NEXT?
AFTER ME.
CAN I USE A GOLF BALL?
OF COURSE, VINCENT.
WHAT'S THIS?
TIGER WOODS?
WHAT? EATING A GOLF BALL?
NO, LOOK AT HIS TEETH.
AND THE TAIL.
THAT MUST BE...
IT'S A SQUIRREL!
YOU GUESSED.
THAT'S IT.
WHO'S NEXT?
ME!
MAY I?
OK. PABLO NEXT.
I'LL GIVE YOU A HARD ONE.
YOU CAN TRY.
WHAT'S THIS, THEN?
HAVEN'T A CLUE!
WHAT A FACE!
HE'S GOT A CURLY TAIL!
AND A SQUINT!
WEIRD!

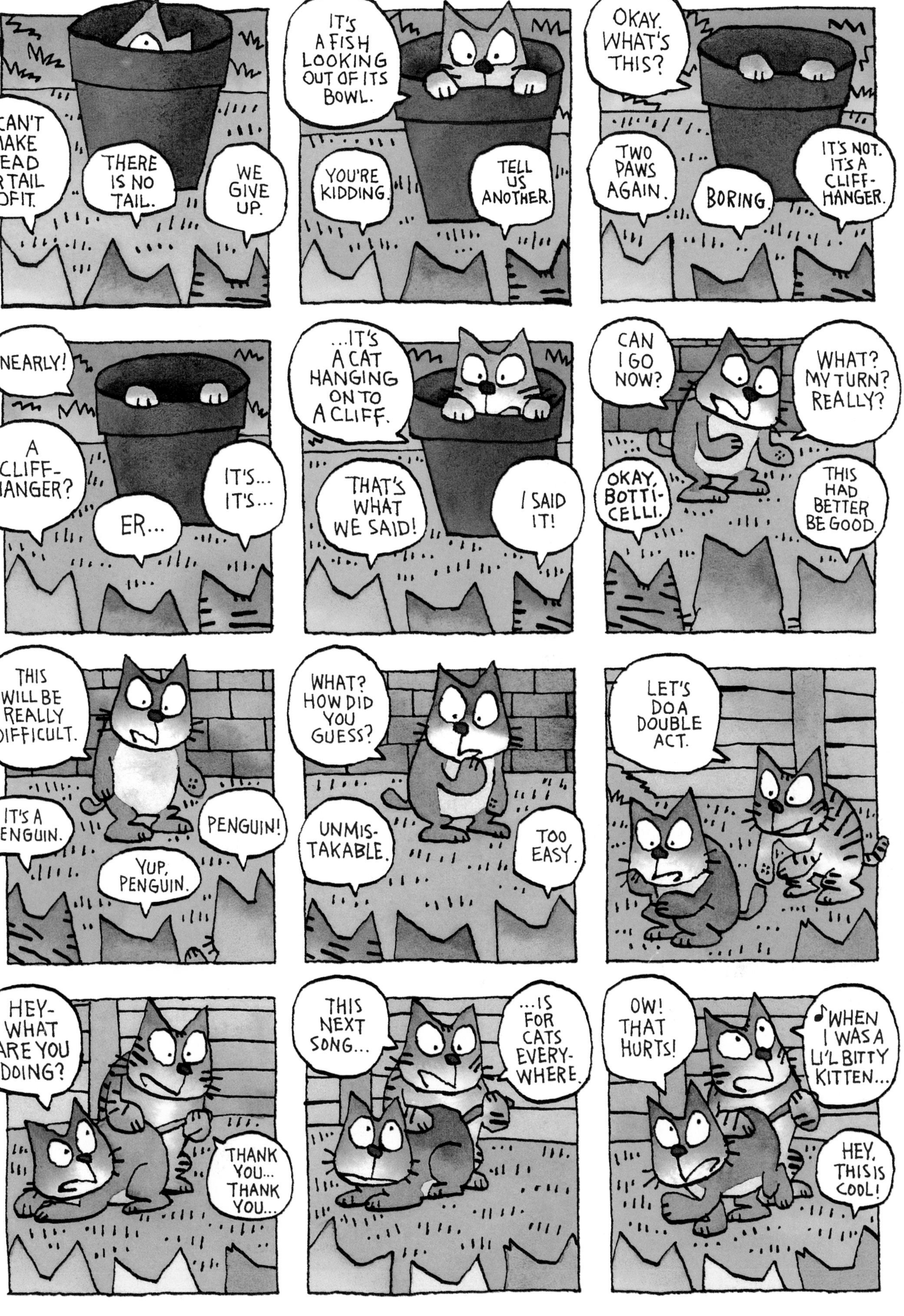
I CAN'T MAKE HEAD OR TAIL OF IT.
THERE IS NO TAIL.
WE GIVE UP.
IT'S A FISH LOOKING OUT OF ITS BOWL.
YOU'RE KIDDING.
TELL US ANOTHER.
OKAY. WHAT'S THIS?
TWO PAWS AGAIN.
BORING.
IT'S NOT. IT'S A CLIFF-HANGER.
NEARLY!
A CLIFF-HANGER?
ER...
IT'S... IT'S...
...IT'S A CAT HANGING ON TO A CLIFF.
THAT'S WHAT WE SAID!
I SAID IT!
CAN I GO NOW?
WHAT? MY TURN? REALLY?
OKAY, BOTTI-CELLI.
THIS HAD BETTER BE GOOD.
THIS WILL BE REALLY DIFFICULT.
IT'S A PENGUIN.
PENGUIN!
YUP, PENGUIN.
WHAT? HOW DID YOU GUESS?
UNMIS-TAKABLE.
TOO EASY.
LET'S DO A DOUBLE ACT.
HEY-WHAT ARE YOU DOING?
THANK YOU... THANK YOU...
THIS NEXT SONG...
...IS FOR CATS EVERY-WHERE.
OW! THAT HURTS!
♪WHEN I WAS A LI'L BITTY KITTEN...
HEY, THIS IS COOL!

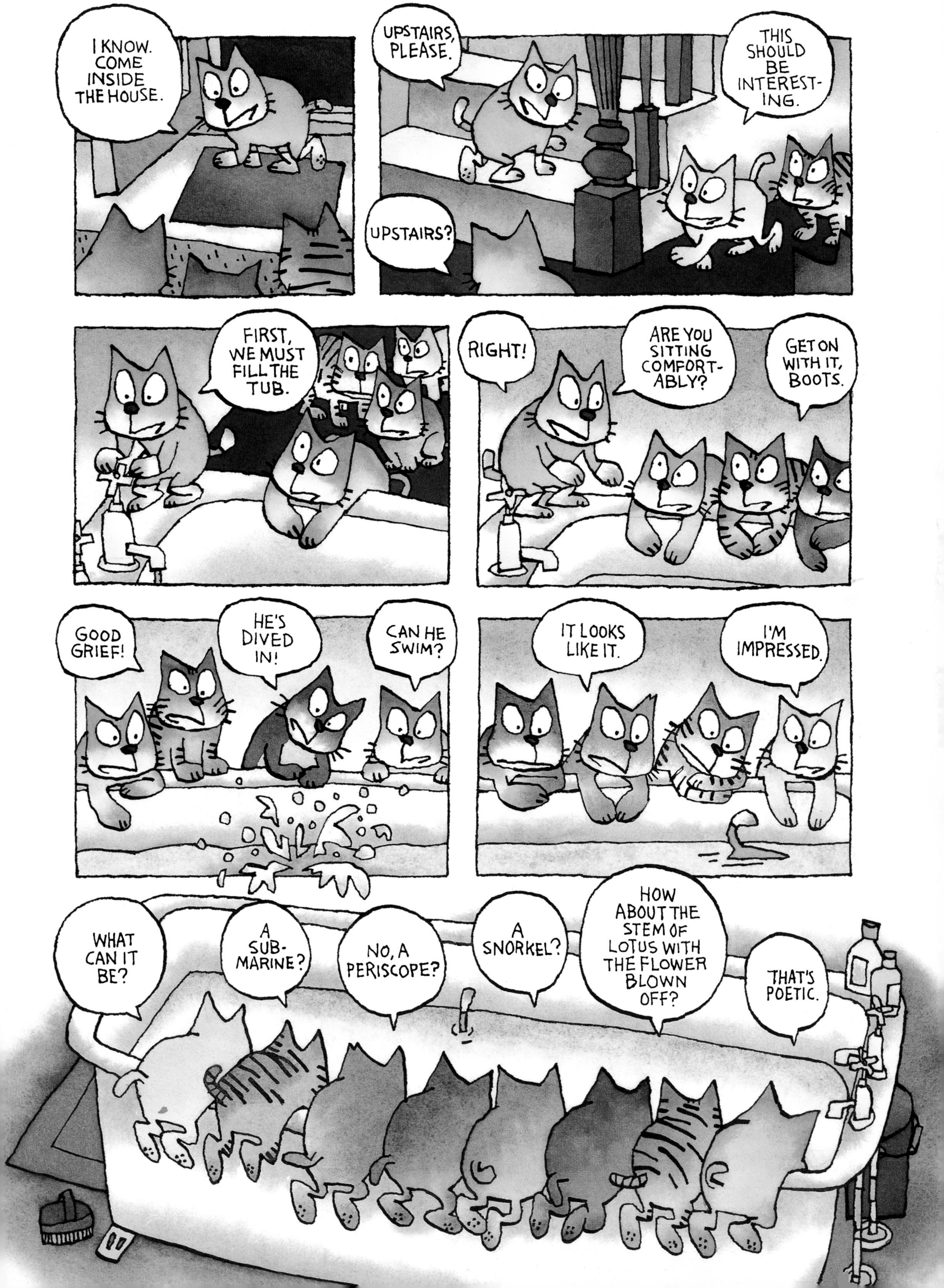
I KNOW. COME INSIDE THE HOUSE.
UPSTAIRS, PLEASE.
THIS SHOULD BE INTEREST-ING.
UPSTAIRS?
FIRST, WE MUST FILL THE TUB.
RIGHT!
ARE YOU SITTING COMFORT-ABLY?
GET ON WITH IT, BOOTS.
GOOD GRIEF!
HE'S DIVED IN!
CAN HE SWIM?
IT LOOKS LIKE IT.
I'M IMPRESSED.
WHAT CAN IT BE?
A SUB-MARINE?
NO, A PERISCOPE?
A SNORKEL?
HOW ABOUT THE STEM OF LOTUS WITH THE FLOWER BLOWN OFF?
THAT'S POETIC.

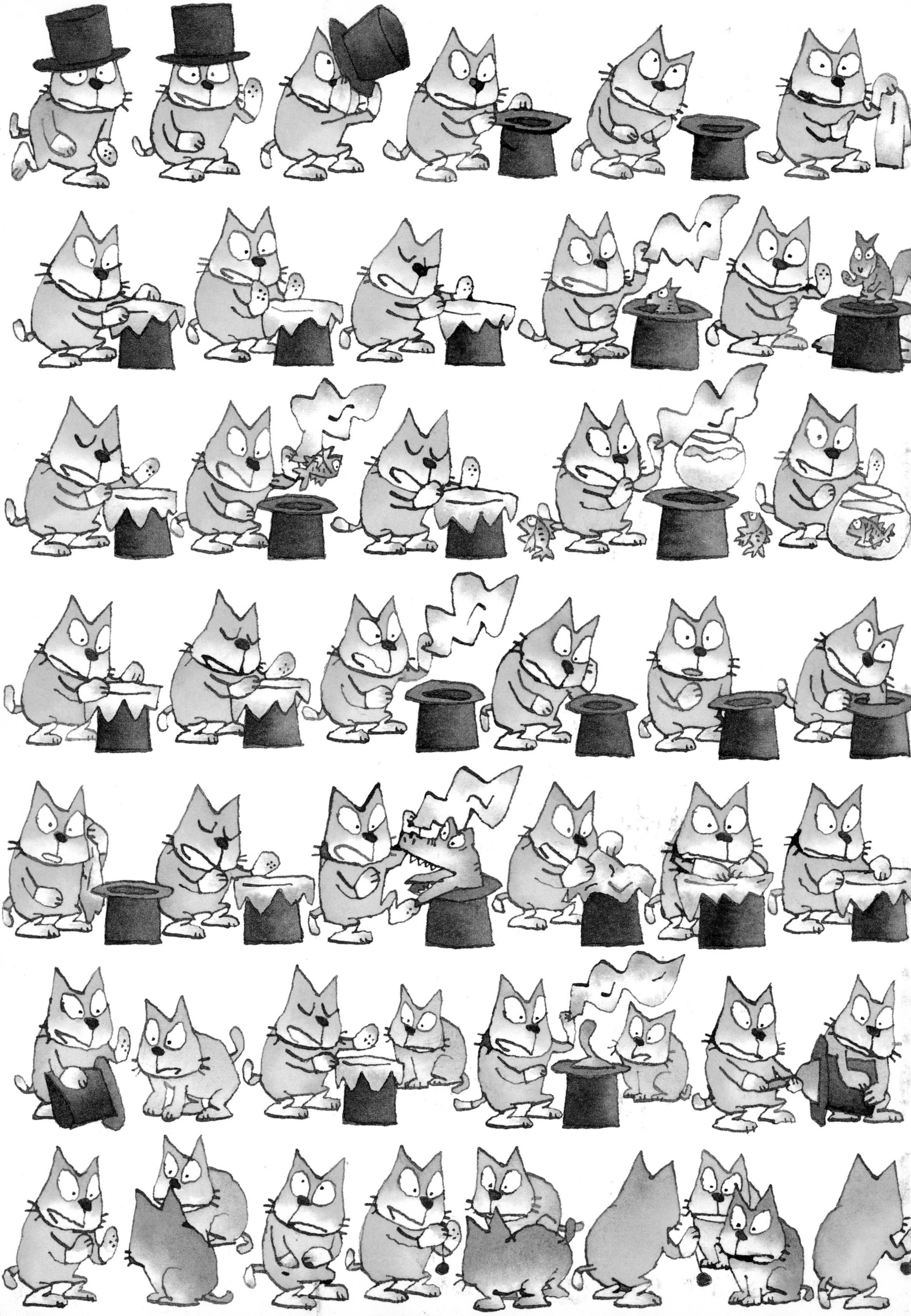